This book belongs to

....

....

....

Johnny Magory in the Magical Wild - First published 2016 by Ballynafagh Press
Johnny Magory and the Game of Rounders - First published 2017 by Ballynafagh Press
Johnny Magory and the Wild Water Race - First published 2017 by Ballynafagh Press

This edition published 2018 by Ballynafagh Press
Ballynafagh, Prosperous, Naas, Co. Kildare, Ireland

ISBN: 978-0-9935792-3-3
Text © 2018 Emma-Jane Leeson
Illustrations © 2018 Kim Shaw

Edited by Aoife Barrett, Dublin, Ireland
Design and Layout by Kim Shaw, Kilkenny, Ireland
Printed in Ireland by KPS Colourprint

Proud members of Guaranteed Irish

Proud partners of CMRF Crumlin. €1 from the sale of this book will be donated to this charity.
Please visit www.CMRF.org for more information

Contents

The Adventures of Johnny Magory

Johnny Magory
in the Magical Wild

Emma-Jane Leeson

I'll tell you a story about Johnny Magory,
And the adventures he has with his trusty dog Ruairi.

He's a clever boy who's six years old,

He's **usually** good,

but he's

sometimes

bold!

Every morning when Johnny wakes up,
He *slurps* his apple juice from his cup.

Apple

He **gobbles** his porridge with

jam   or   honey,

He doesn't mind which - they're both so **yummy**.

And when he finishes he licks his lips to say,

"That was **grand** Mammy,
Now what'll we do today?"

Every day they do something new,

Like go to the beach or make-and-do.

But today his Mammy

has to clean their house,

And Johnny **can't** stay

as quiet as a mouse.

So into his old

exploring clothes he jumps,

And out to the garden he goes with a bump!

Johnny's faithful dog Ruairi meets him, with a big

wuff!

He'll play for hours, doing all kinds of funny stuff.

As they're disappearing his Mammy gets a hunch,

And quickly shouts,

Don't forget to come in for lunch!

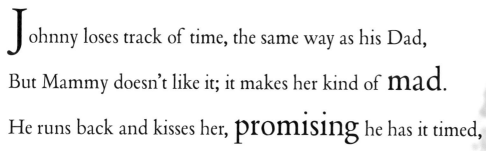

Johnny loses track of time, the same way as his Dad,

But Mammy doesn't like it; it makes her kind of **mad**.

He runs back and kisses her, **promising** he has it timed,

Johnny never means to be late, it just slips his mind!

So off to the bottom of the garden he did bowl,

To his little secret passage down a rabbit hole.

Johnny's hidden tunnel leads into the **magical** wild,

Where he has special friends who'll only talk to a child.

He knows Mr. Fox, Mrs. Squirrel and their families too,

Johnny's their **only** human friend and they **love** him through and through.

And on the Friday morning when Johnny and Ruairi visit,

He hears his friends cheering, so he shouts out;

What is it?

Mr Badger greets him with his usual friendly grin,

We're having a forest party - come and join in!

Now Johnny **loves** to party; he loves to sing and dance,

He knows he's to be back for lunch but he **can't** miss this chance.

So deeper into the forest they go, Mr. Badger behind,

Until Johnny's sparkling eyes see the BIGGEST party he'll ever find!

Giant frogs are playing silver guitars,

As red squirrels blow horns on pink toy cars.

White swans are plucking golden fiddles,

While grey squirrels sing "Hey Diddle Diddle!"

Hedgehogs are doing mad bomb-dives,

And having the time of their lives,

Splashing into the freezing forest lake,

To cheers from the foxes and the corncrakes!

While Johnny dances for hours with the guys,

Ruairi and the frogs keep doing **high fives!**

Then Johnny hears a funny noise and he **knows...**

It's not Ruairi who's singing with the crows.

It's his belly **rumbling** with nothing to munch,
He's played so much he's **missed his lunch!**

He knows he's going to be in trouble -
He feels a bit anxious and in a **muddle.**

Johnny says Goodbye to everyone,

Today has been great - the best fun!

Then Ruairi thanks them for all the craic,

And they run home to get quickly back.

They crawl fast through the secret hole,
With Johnny's clothes as black as coal.

He's heading towards the red back door,
When he hears his Mammy's **big** roar!

Johnny has been very, very bold,
Not doing what he was clearly told.

He said he

meant to be
back on time...

crime!

for his

his room

sent to

...But he's

Later that evening when he's said **sorry** for what he'd done,

Mammy puts him in the bath and *he tells her about the fun...*

From dancing with the **mad** hedgehogs,

And playing **music** with the frogs,

Swimming with the **beautiful** swans,

To waving the fairies' **magic wands!**

Johnny snuggles into his bed,

The day's adventure in his head.

His Mammy kisses him goodnight -

Goodnight Johnny!

And then she turns out the light!

The End

Can you name Johnny Magory's friends?

Why not have your own adventure?

"Johnny Magory in the Magical Wild" was inspired by Ballynafagh Lake near Prosperous in County Kildare, Ireland.

Why not print the free Outdoor Explorer Guide from our website, pack a picnic and take a little explorer on an adventure to try and catch a glimpse of Mr Badger, the swans and all their friends?

25

Johnny Magory
and the Game of Rounders

Emma-Jane Leeson

I'll tell you a story about Johnny Magory,
And the  he has with his trusty dog Ruairi.

He's a clever boy who's six years old,

He's **usually** good,

but he's

sometimes

bold!

Every year around July, it's time for Johnny to go to the bog,
To get the **turf** and bring it home to warm his family

...and the dog!

In wintertime in Ireland, it can be very, **icy cold,**
So, you cut your turf from the peat, a tradition from old.

Johnny gets his exploring clothes, his **wellies** and his orange **hat**,

He helps his Mammy pack **sandwiches** and some **drinks** to go with that.

With sun cream on and insect spray, they all hop into the Jeep,

And with trusty Ruairi strapped in too, they head off with a ...

Beep-Beep!

Once they arrive, Mammy and Daddy waste no time,

Getting to work, footing the turf up and down the line!

And as Johnny is helping,

he hears a familiar sound,

He knows exactly who it is

before he even turns around.

It's Finn the hare, his good old friend, boxing the air,

He gestures to Johnny and Ruairi to follow him if they dare!

Finn Hare is super-quick as they chase him through the purple heather,
They run so fast the bog cotton rises as if it's stormy weather.
They jump the ditches and climb the piles as quickly as they can,
"Where's Finn Hare taking us?" Johnny wonders, "what's his plan?"

They hear cheering in the distance, it sounds like tons of fun,

Johnny and Ruairi can't wait to find out what's at the end of this run.

They race around a gorse bush and stop dead in their tracks;

All their animal friends are there, holding red baseball bats!

They're having a game of **rounders** with batters, bases and the rest,

Lord Stag is the
pitcher, Ms Squirrel on his back -
teamwork at its best!

Johnny **loves** rounders, he can't believe his **good luck**,

He asks the guys,

Can I join in?

Of course!

they say,

line up!

Lord Stag and Ms Squirrel **fire** the sliothar,

Johnny **belts** it with his bat,

And off he runs **as fast as he can**, around the first and second mat.

He's heading towards the **third base** and Johnny's pretty sure he's safe,
But Mr Frog **catches** the ball and he has his leg in the right place!

You're out! he shouts to Johnny, "hard luck, mo chara, he chatters.

Not to worry, grins Johnny, "it's playing, not winning, that matters!"

Mr Frog is next up to take the bat and he really **belts** the ball,

Ms Grouse and Hen Harrier **scramble** to catch it, hoping not to fall.

Their eyes are busy
in the air and not
on the ground,

They **tumble** into each other and feathers **flutter** around!

And when Lord Stag gets up to bat, he does it with a *mighty swoop,*

He's so **eager** to get to first base that he

trips

over

his

hoof!

Bump!

Finn Hare is quick as a flash
and gets the fastest ever **home run,**
By **zipping** by all the bases,
to huge **cheers** from everyone!

The hours are **flying** by because Johnny is having such fun,

The dragonflies are **dancing** to celebrate each home run.

But Ruairi has **super hearing** and he can hear a faint shout, It doesn't take him long to realise it's Mammy and Daddy giving out!

"Woof! Woof!"

It's time to go. Mammy was **yelling** for them.

"Oh no,"
says Johnny,

I'm going to be in trouble again!

42

43

Finn Hare brings them back to where they first set out,
Johnny sees his Ma and Da searching **frantically** about.

He gets into a bit of trouble for not doing his work;
It's all hands on deck when you're **footing the turf!**

He says he's "really sorry" but he winks at Ruairi with a grin,

How could he have passed up a game of rounders with Finn?!

Mammy lays out the picnic blanket and Daddy pours the tea flask,

They sit down to have their lunch in the beautiful purple moor grass.

The End

Can you name Johnny Magory's friends?

Why not have your own adventure?

"Johnny Magory and the Game of Rounders" was inspired by the beautiful raised bogs of County Kildare, Ireland.

Why not print a free Rounders Guide from the website, pack a picnic and a sliotar and take a little explorer on an adventure to try and catch a glimpse of Finn Hare, Lord Stag and all their friends?

Johnny Magory
and the Wild Water Race

Emma-Jane Leeson

I'll tell you a story about Johnny Magory,

His sister Lily-May and their trusty dog Ruairi.

The clever two are three and seven years old,

They're **usually** good

but they're

sometimes

bold!

On most summer evenings, the family take a walk,

Down by the Grand Canal where they **sing** and **talk**.

The **midges** are out in force taking **bites** from everyone,

But nobody really minds because they're having so much fun!

They see their Grandad Paddy making  flowerpots for his boat.

Johnny and Lily-May run over and snuggle into his old coat.

"Sure look it," Paddy says,

Will you join me on a cruise?
There's a problem with a lock gate
and there's no time to lose!

51

Johnny loves his Grandad's barge where he can wander and roam,

There's a kitchen, a bathroom and two bedrooms in the floating home.

Mammy puts on the life jackets, as Paddy cranks the engine to life.

The kids love the orange life vests, with the white reflective stripe.

The canals were made years ago for barges,

Paddy shouts.

For a **path through Ireland**,
so merchants could get about.
Their faithful **horses** would pull
the barges full of cargo along.
The men would **laugh** and **talk**
and **sing** a boatman's song.

OLAGH

Johnny **loves** listening to Paddy as he stands and helps him steer,
And he learns more about Ireland's canals every single year!

53

Johnny spots **Mr Otter** waving like mad from the bank,
He somersaults into the water from the diving plank!

We're going to have a race, will you and Ruairi join in?

That'll be grand, says Johnny. Sure we might even win!

COOL

Ahoy, there!

shouts Paddy, as they approach the broken lock.

He ties up "Coolagh" the barge on the black wooden block.

Mammy and Lily-May pick **blackberries**

as the men start fixing the gate.

Daddy **warns** Johnny and Ruairi,

Don't go **wandering** and come back late.

I promise I'll be back on time,

Johnny says to his **smiling** dad.

He never **means** to get in trouble or to make his parents mad!

Mr Otter leads them down the steep bank to a special place,

To a stream that runs under the canal, to have a water race.

The **Duck** family are there with **Heron** and lots of frogs.
Dusty the old **barge horse** shows
them a **raft** made of logs.

Dusty takes the thick rope,
one of a **mighty** Irish team,
He's going to pull Johnny and
Ruairi down the shallow stream.

58

Mr Otter has a **fine boat,** made from moss and twigs and rope,

The ducks' boat is made of lily-pads and is the **fastest** they hope!

Heron is at the starting line, getting them ready to **begin.**

Ms Swan is at the **finish line,**

to see who will win.

Heron flaps his wings,

On your marks, get set, GO!

The race **begins** with everybody lined up in a row.

Mrs Pike joins in too, so the stream is pretty **tight**,

But **steady** Dusty pulls them along, a job he's done all his life.

Mr Otter's boat gets tangled up in the thick bullrush,

The ducks are so busy **quacking** they sail into a bush!

Mr Trout and Mrs Pike swim so **fast** they are nearly there,

But they see a swarm of flies and start **feasting** elsewhere!

Faithful Dusty keeps on going, one slow step at a time,

Johnny shouts **"Hooray"**, as they pass the finish line!

Ms Swan says,

You're the winners, there's no shadow of a doubt!

Johnny rubs the horse's ears and laughs,

We're happy out!

Ruairi hears Mammy shouting, so they have to make a run,

Back up to the canal to tell Lily-May about all the fun!

Mammy is fierce angry as Johnny appears from up the slope,

You put the heart crossways on me!

she says, untying the rope.

"I'm really sorry," says Johnny, "I didn't mean to be late."

"Ah don't worry," says Paddy, "we've just finished the gate."

Everyone gets back on the barge and Johnny sits beside Lily-May,

And as Mammy gets **berries** and **ice-cream**, he tells her about his day.

Lily-May hears about the race and all his **exciting** friends,

He fills her in on Dusty, Heron, Ms Swan and how it ends.

Lily-May **can't wait** until she's old enough to go too,

I'm dying to join Johnny and Ruairi on the adventures they do!

Whist, macushla,

Mammy says to her small daughter.

You'll have **many** more years to enjoy life on the water!

When they get home, they brush their teeth and climb into their beds,

And dreams of Ireland's magical waterways fill their tired heads.

Johnny can't help wondering what his next adventure will be,

And he promises Lily-May,

I'll bring you along with me!

Can you name Johnny Magory's friends?

Why not have your own adventure?

"Johnny Magory and the Wild Water Race" was inspired by the river Slate that flows under the Grand Canal near Lowtown Marina in county Kildare, Ireland.

Why not pack a picnic and take a little explorer on an adventure to try and catch a glimpse of Mr Otter, Heron and all their friends?